Cambridge English Readers

Level 3

Series editor: Philip Prowse

Wild Country

Margaret Johnson

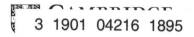

CAMBRIDGE UNIVERSITY PRESS

Cambridge, New York, Melbourne, Madrid, Cape Town, Singapore, São Paulo, Delhi

Cambridge University Press
The Edinburgh Building, Cambridge CB2 8RU, UK

www.cambridge.org
Information on this title: www.cambridge.org/9780521713672

First published 2008

Margaret Johnson has asserted her right to be identified as the Author of the Work in
accordance with the Copyright, Design and Patents Act 1988.

Printed in India by Thomson Press (India) Limited

A catalogue record of this book is available from the British Library.

ISBN 978-0-521-71367-2 paperback
ISBN 978-0-521-71368-9 paperback plus audio CD pack

Contents

Characters

Tess: a tour leader who works for Wild Country, a walking holiday company
Grant: another Wild Country tour leader
Ellen: a Canadian woman on holiday
David: a sixty-year-old man on holiday
James and Sarah: a honeymoon couple on holiday
Astrid: an eighteen-year-old Scandinavian woman on holiday

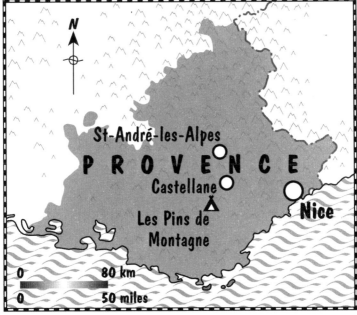

Chapter 1 *The flower market mistake*

The woman in the red dress was holding some large yellow flowers to her face. Behind her, there were lots more flowers – big flowers, small flowers, flowers of every possible colour.

I was very pleased I'd got up early to see Nice's famous flower market. It was beautiful, and it helped me to forget that I wasn't going to have a nice day. Or a nice ten days.

Grant Cooper! *Grant Cooper*! I couldn't believe I was going to work with that man for ten days. It was going to be horrible. But I wouldn't think about it until I had to. And here, in the market, I could almost forget.

There was colour all around me – not just the flowers, but also the people buying them in their summer clothes. Even the buildings behind the market were colourful – red and orange with blue windows. What a lovely picture it would make, if I only had my paints with me. But I *did* have a pencil somewhere. I could do a quick drawing. I still had a few minutes before I had to leave for the airport.

I found the pencil in the bottom of my shoulder bag, together with an old letter. Soon my pencil was moving quickly over the back of the letter as I began to draw the woman in the red dress. She was smelling some red flowers now, and her hair was very blonde in the sunshine. As I drew what I saw, I quickly forgot about everything else. The woman buying the flowers obviously knew the flower seller. They were talking and laughing together, and I had lots of time to work on my picture.

I don't know how long I stood there. I only know that the next time I looked at my watch, it was nine o'clock. Nine o'clock! I only had thirty minutes to get to the airport. Oh no, I was going to be late. Again.

But before I could put the pencil and paper back into my bag, I felt something soft against my legs. It was a small brown dog, and he was on his own. 'Hello, boy,' I said. 'Are you lost?'

The dog seemed to smile up at me, and I reached out to touch it. The dog smiled again, and then … it bit me!

I screamed and jumped quickly back from the dog. Too quickly. There was a very loud crash behind me.

'*Mademoiselle!*' shouted an angry voice.

I turned round to see flowers all over the ground. 'I'm sorry,' I said. 'That dog – it bit me!'

'What dog?' asked the angry flower seller.

'Well, that one,' I said, but when I looked down, the dog had disappeared. 'It was here a minute ago,' I said, turning to look. Unfortunately, I turned so quickly that my shoulder bag flew through the air and crashed into some more flowers.

'*Mademoiselle!*' shouted the flower seller again.

'I'm sorry,' I started to say, but then I noticed that things were about to get even worse. A river of dirty water from the flowers was moving very quickly towards the blonde woman's expensive white summer shoes.

'*Madame!*' I shouted, but it was too late.

'My shoes!' cried the blonde woman.

'My flowers!' cried the flower seller.

I held my hand up to show what the dog had done.

'My finger!' I cried, but neither the flower seller nor the blonde woman was interested in my hurt finger.

After I'd given a lot of money to the flower seller for her flowers, and to the blonde woman to clean her dirty shoes, I caught a bus to the airport. I was feeling fed up. It wasn't the best start to a new tour. But then my tours never did seem to go well.

I'd been a tour leader for Wild Country, my father's walking holiday company, for a year. In that time I'd been late meeting a group at the airport several times. I'd also lost my wallet, with all the money to buy food for the tour group for a week in it. And, of course, everybody who worked for Wild Country knew about the time I'd taken a group to the wrong town on the wrong day. They'd all missed their plane home. Now, *that* was a very famous mistake.

My mistakes were so famous in the company that doing something wrong was called 'doing a Tess Marriot'. I think it was Grant Cooper who started saying that, actually – horrible man.

And now my father had arranged for me to work with Grant Cooper on this tour. He thought I would learn something from Grant – something to make me a better tour leader. I thought my father was wrong. I was just too different to Grant; and I didn't *want* to be like him anyway.

After thirty minutes in a hot bus with these thoughts going round and round my head I felt very fed up. Which was the opposite of how I should be when I meet a group at the start of a holiday.

'A tour leader should smile as often as possible.' That's what it said in the book I was given when I started the job. 'At the beginning of a tour, holidaymakers are often tired from their journeys. They may also be worried about what the other people on the holiday will be like. A smile from you makes everybody feel better.'

So as I entered the airport building I tried to put a smile on my face. But it was difficult to keep it there as I tried, without luck, to find my group.

'Wild Country, Walking in Provence?' I asked any group of more than four people, but they all looked at me as if I was mad. I was beginning to think I'd got the time wrong or come to the wrong airport when I saw *him* – Grant Cooper. My heart immediately gave a jump, and not just because I was nervous about being late. I didn't like Grant, but he was very good-looking. I'd liked the look of him when I first met him. But then I'd spoken to him, and all that changed. I just didn't find him easy to get on with. Every time he spoke to me I felt he was laughing at me. It made me so mad I wanted to scream.

As I got closer, I could see that Grant had already found the group. There was nothing else to do but walk up to them with a big Wild Country smile on my face.

'Hello, everybody,' I said. 'I'm Tess Marriot, one of your tour leaders. I hope you had a good journey?'

'Hello, Tess,' Grant said. 'Did you get lost on your way to the airport?'

My face went red. 'No,' I said. 'I had a bit of an accident. But I'm here now, so perhaps we'd better make our way to the hotel. The Hotel La Tour, isn't it?'

I reached into my shoulder bag for the hotel information, but could only find my drawing of the market. 'Oh,' I said, 'that's not it. I'm sure it's here somewhere.'

'You've probably lost it,' Grant told me. 'But never mind. I have the information here. It's the Hotel des Deux Tours.'

I turned my drawing over. 'Here it is,' I said. 'Hotel des Deux Tours. You're right.'

Grant smiled at me. 'I usually am,' he said. 'Very nice drawing by the way, Tess. Right, everyone, now we're finally all here, let's get on our way. The tour bus is waiting for us outside.'

As I followed everyone out of the airport building I felt as if there must be smoke coming from the top of my head. It was the way I always felt when I was around Grant Cooper. 'Thank you very much, Dad,' I thought. 'Thank you very much!'

Chapter 2 *Please, Dad!*

I sat next to a woman called Ellen on the bus. She was Canadian and she told me she'd been on Wild Country holidays all over the world. She seemed very nice.

As I half listened to her, I looked at the other people in the group. It was a small group – only five people altogether. There was a couple who were kissing or touching each other all the time, and I thought they must be just married and on holiday. A honeymoon couple. They were called James and Sarah, but I knew I'd always think of them as the honeymoon couple. There was also a white-haired man of about sixty and a very beautiful Scandinavian woman of about eighteen with long blonde hair. Astrid, she was called. She'd smiled when we were introduced, but now she was looking out of the window. I thought she looked sad.

The man with the white hair was called David, and he had a walking stick. Grant was talking to him about the mountains. He probably wanted to know if David would be able to do all the walking on the holiday. Wild Country holidays are really for people in good health, because the walks can be difficult. I knew Grant had to ask David about his leg, but I hoped he'd be kind about it. Before he started working for Wild Country, Grant had been a soldier for five years. Sometimes he spoke to tourists as if they were soldiers too. He'd spoken to me like that when we first met, but I wasn't going to let him do it on this tour. Oh, no!

The couple were kissing again. Ellen saw me looking at them. 'Makes you feel a bit sick, doesn't it?' she said softly, and I had to put my hand over my mouth to hide my smile. A tour leader should *not* laugh at the tourists in their group. I didn't need the Wild Country book to tell me that.

'What did you do to your finger?' Ellen asked me, and I saw Grant look over at us with that smile of his.

'Yes,' he said. 'What *did* you do to your finger, Tess?'

'It's a long story,' I said, and turned my head away so I couldn't see him.

But I still heard what he said: 'I thought it might be.' And then he laughed.

When we got to the hotel I phoned my father, while Grant went to the front desk with the group.

'I'm just on my way to a meeting, Tess,' my father said. 'Can I call you back later?'

'This will only take a minute, Dad,' I said. 'I just want to ask you to let me work with someone else. Please. I don't like Grant. We just don't get on well together.'

When he spoke, Dad sounded a bit impatient. 'Oh, Tess,' he said. 'Grant's a good man, and he's very good at his job. You'll learn a lot from him.'

'Listen, Dad,' I started to say, but it was no good.

'Come on, Tess,' he said. 'You'll be OK. After all, when you take over the company you're going to have to get on with everyone, aren't you? Now, I must go. My meeting's about to start. Love you.'

And he was gone.

As I went to join Grant and the group, everyone looked at me. I felt as if they knew what I'd been talking to my father about.

12

'OK, Tess?' Grant asked me, and I smiled as nicely as I could.

'Yes, thank you, Grant,' I said.

'Good,' he said, and then turned to the group. 'Right, you can go up to your rooms for a bit, and we'll meet back down here at twelve o'clock. I'll tell you something about the tour, and then the rest of the day is free for you to do what you like. OK?'

After they'd all gone off to their rooms, Grant and I were left alone.

'I can help you tell them about the tour, if you like,' I offered.

Grant looked at me. 'I didn't think you'd been here before,' he said.

'I haven't led a tour here,' I said, 'but I have been on holiday here. I know the area quite well.'

Grant smiled. 'Well, I think I must know the area a little bit better than you, Tess. I've been leading tours here for over a year now. Anyway, I thought the idea was for you to learn from me.'

My face quickly went red. It was clear that Grant thought it was very funny that my father had sent me to learn from him. 'I don't need to learn how to speak to a group,' I told him. 'I don't have any problems doing that.'

'No?' Grant said. 'Well, of course, do add anything if you think it will be helpful, Tess.'

From the way he said it, I knew he didn't think anything I said to the group *would* be helpful.

'See you back here in an hour.' Grant turned to leave, then looked back. 'Oh, and Tess, if you do leave the hotel, please don't get lost.'

He was laughing as he walked away. As for me, that smoke was starting to come out of the top of my head again, I knew it was! It was going to be a *very* long ten days.

Chapter 3   *Shopping with Grant*

'First thing tomorrow, we drive to St-André-les-Alpes,' Grant said. 'From there we start a six-hour walk through the forest to Castellane,' Grant told the group.

'You'll *love* Castellane,' I added. 'It's so beautiful. There's a lovely river, and mountains everywhere.'

Grant gave me a look. 'Thank you, Tess,' he said. 'While we're in Castellane you can climb up to the top of Robion mountain, which is one thousand, six hundred and sixty metres high …'

'Or there are some nice restaurants with tables outside if you want to just *look* at Robion with some good food and a glass of wine,' I said.

Grant's voice sounded cross. 'Next day it's an early start as we climb above the Verdon river, where the mountains of Cadières de Brandis are one thousand metres high …'

'The colours are beautiful,' I told the group. 'The river is so blue through the trees, and the mountains seem to be looking down on us like people …'

Ellen started to laugh. 'Are you two sure you're talking about the same holiday?' she asked.

Grant looked at me crossly. 'Just what I was thinking, Ellen,' he said.

'We don't have to carry our bags, do we?' asked David worriedly.

'No,' I said quickly, before Grant could answer. 'Your bags go by bus.'

'Don't worry; you won't have much to carry,' said Grant. 'Just the things you need during the day – water, lunch, money; things like that. Everything else goes in the bus,' Grant went on. 'The tents you'll be sleeping in, your sleeping bags, the cooking things – everything.' Grant looked at his watch. 'Right. The rest of today is free for you to look around Nice. Tess and I need to go shopping for food for the tour, so we'll meet you back here tomorrow morning at eight o'clock to set off for St-André-les-Alpes.' He stood up and began walking away, calling to me as if I were a dog. 'Come on, Tess.'

* * *

I had no idea why Grant wanted me to go shopping with him, because half the time he was walking ahead of me. Even when I did catch up with him, he didn't agree with anything I wanted to buy.

'That cheese is no good, Tess,' Grant said.

'Why not? It tastes lovely,' I replied.

'True, but it'll also smell horrible after a few days in the sun,' Grant went on.

'Not peaches, Tess,' he said.

'What's wrong with peaches?' I asked.

'They're too soft. Apples are better,' he replied.

And so on. By the time we'd finished our shopping, I wasn't feeling very happy at all. The fact that I secretly knew Grant was right about everything made it worse. I did like smelly cheese and soft peaches. But I really only wanted to buy them because he didn't want me to.

'Right,' said Grant after we'd taken the shopping back to the hotel. 'That's me finished for the day. I'm meeting someone this afternoon.'

It was obvious from his smile that the 'someone' was a woman.

As if *I* was interested. 'See you tomorrow then,' I said and turned away.

'Yes,' said Grant. 'At eight o'clock.'

He'd said the words 'eight o'clock' loudly, and I turned back. 'I can tell the time, you know,' I said, but I could see from his face he wasn't sure that this was true.

'Good,' he said laughingly, but when I started to leave, he called after me again.

'Look, Tess.'

I turned round again. 'What is it now?'

'I didn't ask to work with you, and I know you didn't ask to work with me. But here we are, so shall we at least try to get on with each other?'

I looked back at him crossly. *He* was the one who was doing everything he could to make me angry all the time. He was the one who was talking about my mistakes and laughing at me! 'I'll try if you try,' I said, but I didn't like the smile he gave me.

'Of course I'll try, Tess,' he said. Then he gave me a little wave and walked off. Probably to meet his 'someone'. Poor woman. She didn't know what she was getting herself into.

As for me, I went back to my hotel room to work on a painting of the woman in the market. Or at least that was what I wanted to do, but I couldn't keep my mind on my work. Grant and some of the things he'd said to me kept getting in the way. Why did he enjoy making me angry so much? It had always been the same, ever since we'd first met. He thought I only had my job because Wild Country was my father's company.

I left my painting and took a glass of orange juice over to the window. The street below was busy with people enjoying the sunshine as they looked in shop windows at expensive fashions. But I didn't really see them. I was still thinking about Grant.

The trouble was, he was right. I *did* still only have my job because Wild Country was Dad's company. If it hadn't been his company, I'd have been out after the wrong airport mistake, I was sure. And the truth was, I wasn't very comfortable with that fact. Which was why Grant made me so angry when he talked about it.

I didn't want to be a bad tour leader. In fact, I didn't want to be a tour leader at all. I wanted to be an artist. But Dad wouldn't hear of it. His father, my grandfather, had been an artist. But the family had been very poor because grandfather hadn't sold many pictures.

Dad didn't want me to be poor. He'd worked very hard all his life, and now he was rich and Wild Country was doing very well. I'm his only child, and since Mum died fifteen years ago Dad and I have always been very close. We may be very different, but we love each other very much. I wanted to please him, but sometimes it was very hard. I wanted to be an artist so very much. I wanted to do something I was good at. And I just knew I would never be good at being the manager of Wild Country, which is what Dad wanted me to be.

Oh well. For now, at least, there was nothing I could do about it. So I went back to my painting of the woman in the market, and after a few minutes I forgot about Grant and Dad. I forgot about everything except colour and light and paint.

Chapter 4 *The tour begins*

To be sure that I wasn't late the next day, I got up early and was down at breakfast by seven o'clock.

Ellen was already there, and when she waved to me, I took my breakfast over to her table.

'Morning,' I said. 'May I join you?'

She smiled at me. 'Please do.'

I sat down and put sugar in my coffee. 'Did you enjoy your afternoon in Nice?' I asked.

Ellen nodded. 'Oh yes,' she said. 'I did lots of shopping. It's a very good thing our bags go by bus.' She looked at me. 'How did you and Grant do with *your* shopping?'

Something about the way she was looking at me made my face go red. 'Fine,' I said, and she smiled.

'He's a very handsome man,' she said.

'Is he?' I said.

'Don't you think so?' continued Ellen.

'I haven't really thought about it,' I said, which of course wasn't the truth. I just wanted to talk about something else. 'Are you looking forward to today's walk?' I asked.

Ellen smiled again. 'Yes,' she said, 'very much.'

At that moment Grant came into the restaurant, and both Ellen and I looked his way. He wasn't alone. A tall woman with black hair was holding his hand.

'Who is *that?*' Ellen asked me, not sounding pleased.

Grant saw us and called over, 'Good morning, ladies. Beautiful morning, isn't it?'

'That,' I told Ellen, 'must be his French girlfriend.'

'Is she coming on the tour with us?' asked Ellen.

'I have no idea,' I said.

But in the end the woman didn't join us when the bus set off for St-André-les-Alpes. Grant kissed her goodbye and then he got on the bus. The woman stood and watched us drive away. She looked sad.

Ellen was sitting in the seat next to me. 'Do you think he'll see her again?' she whispered, but I didn't want to think about it.

'Who knows?' I said.

Grant was sitting at the front, next to the driver. He turned round to look at us. 'OK, as we're driving along, I'll tell you something about what we're going to do,' he said.

Grant stopped to smile at everyone, and everyone – except me – smiled back.

'As you'll know from the holiday information, on this tour we spend two nights *au sauvage*,' he went on.

David spoke up. 'I read that, but I wasn't sure what it meant,' he said.

'It means we put our tents up in the wild,' Grant told him. 'We won't be using a campsite, and we won't be near any towns or villages, so there'll be no bars or restaurants.'

'And no toilets?' Ellen asked him with a smile.

Grant smiled back. 'That's correct, Ellen,' he said. 'No toilets. But don't worry, there are trees to hide behind and lots of earth.'

Astrid didn't look very happy about that and, to tell the truth, I didn't blame her. But actually Astrid didn't ever look very happy. I made a note in my mind to have a quiet talk with her soon. The poor woman looked as if she wanted to cry all the time. Something must be wrong.

'Tonight we have both toilets and a very good restaurant, you'll be glad to hear,' Grant continued. 'OK, one more thing before I let you enjoy the rest of the journey. When we stop for the night, you'll all need to learn how to put your tents up. I'll show you how to do it tonight, but after that you're on your own. Don't worry, it isn't difficult. But it's important to put your tent up safely, or it could blow away if the wind gets strong.'

'OK.' Grant looked at us all. 'Does anybody have any questions? No? How about you, Tess? Anything you want to add? About all the beautiful colours we'll be seeing perhaps?'

He was having another joke at me, I knew. But this time he wasn't going to make me cross. I smiled at him sweetly. 'No, thank you, Grant,' I said. 'I think you've told us everything we need to know for now.'

Grant turned around, and I felt Ellen touch me with her elbow. 'Isn't he wonderful?' she said. 'I could eat him, I really could!'

'No, thank you,' I thought. 'I don't want my stomach to hurt.'

Chapter 5 *Colours and conversation*

We began our six-hour walk from St-André-les-Alpes at about eleven o'clock. Soon we were beginning to climb up a very big hill. Grant was at the front with Ellen, and they looked deep in conversation. The honeymoon couple were behind them, holding hands, and then came Astrid, David and myself.

As I walked I could hear the sound of Ellen laughing, and I thought she was probably already letting Grant know how wonderful he was. Grant's head would be very big by the end of the holiday. Though come to think of it, it was already quite big. Women always seemed to be throwing themselves at him. I had no idea why. Appearance wasn't everything. You only had to spend a few minutes with the man to know that.

I decided to talk to David, and get to know him better.

'Going uphill is hard work, isn't it?' I started, but actually David seemed to be doing OK. Better than me, in fact.

'I find it more difficult going downhill with my leg,' he told me.

'Do you?' I said. 'What did you do to your leg, if you don't mind me asking?'

'I crashed my motorbike when I was twenty,' he told me.

'Oh,' I said, 'how awful!'

David smiled at me. 'It was my own fault. I was riding badly,' he said. 'And anyway it was a long time ago. I can't really remember what it's like not to have a bad leg any more. It certainly doesn't stop me doing what I want to do.'

'I can see that,' I said. David was walking quickly, much more quickly than me.

'Actually,' he said, looking back at me, 'do you mind if I go on ahead? My leg hurts in the afternoons, but it's fine in the morning.'

'Of course not,' I said, feeling stupid. As one of the tour leaders I should be able to climb these hills with no problem. But actually I was feeling a bit tired. Well, it was a very big hill. As I'd told Grant, I'd been here before on holiday. But it hadn't been a holiday like this. I'd come with a friend, and we'd driven everywhere in her car.

After about half an hour my legs really hurt and I was very hot. I stopped for a moment to rest, and looked down the hill towards St-André-les-Alpes. The town looked very small, and the light was beautiful. There was sunshine on the buildings, and the roofs were an orange-red colour. The hills around the town were dark though, and I saw that the sky was full of large, black clouds.

'Tess!' A voice shouted to me from further up the hill.

I looked up to see Grant – and the rest of the group – looking down at me.

'What are you doing?' Grant's voice was angry.

'Er … just looking at the colours,' I shouted back, and began to walk again.

When I reached the group, Grant's face looked like one of the black clouds I'd just seen in the sky. 'When she's not a tour leader, Tess is an artist,' Grant told everyone. He thought people would laugh, but they didn't.

'Really?' said Ellen and David together. Even the honeymoon couple – James and Sarah – looked interested.

'We're looking for some pictures for our new home,' they told me. 'A picture of this area would be really good.'

'Well,' I said, pleased, 'if I have time, I'll do one for you.'

Grant's face looked even more like a black cloud than ever. 'Can we continue walking, please?' he said, 'if you've seen enough colours for now, Tess.'

Sarah laughed behind her hand, and I smiled at her. 'I'll talk to you and James about it this evening, Sarah,' I told her.

We began walking again. Ten minutes later it began to rain. Very heavily. Within seconds, those people in the group who hadn't brought their raincoats with them – which was Sarah and James, Astrid and of course me – were wet through.

I caught up with Astrid. 'We'll soon dry out when the sun comes out again,' I told her with a smile. 'It gets so hot in the south of France.'

'I don't like the heat,' Astrid said unhappily.

'Oh,' I said. So why had she decided to come on holiday to a hot part of the world when she didn't like the heat? Astrid's hair was very blonde. Her skin was very fair too. I hoped she had a sun hat with her. 'Well, we'll be walking through the forest very soon,' I said.

The rain stopped when we reached the forest. Unfortunately, the trees shut out the sunshine, so those of us with wet clothes walked along very uncomfortably. Even my walking shoes had rain in them. I could feel the water between my toes every time I put my foot down. It was horrible.

Ahead of me, Sarah and James were laughing together. They didn't seem to mind about being wet, and it was easy to think of them in thirty years' time telling their grandchildren about it. 'When we went on our honeymoon, it rained and rained and rained …' I thought about trying to talk to them about the painting they wanted. Then they looked at each other and kissed – *again* – and I decided to leave it for a while.

So I turned to Astrid. 'They look very happy, don't they?' I said with a smile, but Astrid didn't smile back.

'Yes, they do,' she said in her sad voice. 'Though I cannot understand why they are on this holiday. I would want to be alone if I was just married.'

'Yes,' I said. 'I think I would too.' I smiled at her again. 'What made you choose this holiday, Astrid?' I asked. 'Do you like walking?'

'Yes,' she said, her voice sounding tired. 'I do like walking, but I did not.'

I didn't understand. 'Sorry?' I said. 'You did not what?'

'I did not choose this holiday,' she explained. 'My boyfriend chose it.'

'Oh, I see,' I said, interested. 'And why couldn't he come with you?'

'Well,' Astrid said, her voice sounding strange. 'He decided to go to Australia. With … with his new girlfriend.'

When I saw that Astrid was crying, I wished I hadn't asked her about the holiday. I'd only wanted to make conversation, but now I seemed to have made things worse. 'I'm sorry, Astrid,' I said, and she looked at me.

'So am I!' she said. '*Australia*. Australia is a country I dreamed of going to with my boyfriend Christian. But he wanted to come here. And I wanted only to be with him. So I said yes. And then one week ago he told me it was all over between us. He had met a new woman and he did not love me any more. It is not *fair*.'

Ahead of us, Sarah and James were still laughing, their arms around each other as they walked. Astrid stopped walking and put her hands to her face. She was crying really loudly now, and everyone, including Grant, turned round to see what was wrong.

'Oh, very good work, Tess,' I told myself angrily, putting my hand on Astrid's shoulder. 'Very good work indeed!'

Chapter 6 *Tents and café bars*

I'd like to be able to say the day got better after this, but I can't, because it didn't. Astrid stopped crying, but she was quiet and unhappy all day. Just after lunch it started to rain again, and it didn't stop all afternoon. By the time we got near our campsite, the people with raincoats were also wet. And even though he didn't say anything, I could tell David's leg was hurting. Even Ellen, James and Sarah had stopped smiling.

'I'll go on ahead and meet the driver; the bus should be there by now,' Grant said. 'Just walk straight on, Tess. You can't miss the campsite. It's called Les Pins de Montagne, and it's about two kilometres away, just through the village.' With that, he walked quickly away, leaving us to follow.

We stood in a wet group under some trees, watching him until he went around the corner, and then I turned to look at everybody. 'OK,' I said with a smile, 'anybody know any jokes to make us feel better?' There were a few smiles, but nobody said anything. 'OK,' I said, 'I'll start. Where do horses go when they're ill?' I waited a few moments before I told them. 'To the horse-pital!'

'That's a very bad joke, Tess,' Ellen said, but most people were smiling.

'OK,' I said, 'how about this one? What game do cows play at parties? Moosical chairs!'

'That one's even worse!' Ellen said, but everyone laughed because the joke was so bad. As we walked on through the rain other people told their own jokes. By the time we reached the village, we were feeling happier and when we reached a café bar, Ellen stopped.

'I don't know about anybody else, but I'd really like to go in there for a nice hot cup of coffee,' she said.

The others agreed. 'OK,' I said, 'I'm sure a quick cup of coffee would be fine.'

The café bar was warm with comfortable chairs. Even though it was August, there was a nice fire burning. 'I made a fire because of this weather,' the café owner told us. 'This summer is the wettest in this area for fifty years!'

'Thank you for telling us that,' said Ellen.

We sat near the fire to dry off, and after we'd finished our coffee, nobody wanted to move. The café owner came over to take our empty cups.

'Can I get you anything else?' he asked. 'More coffee perhaps?'

Ellen looked at her cup. 'Just one more coffee before we go?' she said, looking at me hopefully.

'We have food as well,' the café owner told us.

'I *am* hungry,' said Sarah.

'Me too,' said James. 'It's a long time since lunch.'

'Ages,' agreed Ellen. 'In fact, I don't think I could walk another step until I've eaten something.'

'Me neither,' said David, picking up a menu.

I looked out of the window. It was still raining, but I thought about Grant waiting at Les Pins de Montagne for us. I knew we really should be going. We had to put the tents up. But by now even Astrid had a menu in her hands. I couldn't *make* them all come, and the weather was awful. Grant should understand.

I looked in my bag for my phone. It wasn't there. I looked in my jacket pocket. It wasn't there either. Perhaps I'd left it in my other jacket pocket, or my suitcase. I'd have to walk to the campsite to tell Grant what was happening.

I stood up. 'I'd better go and tell Grant where we are,' I said. 'See you all back here later.'

'OK,' they said happily. 'See you later.'

But as I walked through the rain towards Les Pins de Montagne I became more and more sure that Grant would *not* understand. He'd told me to bring the group to Les Pins de Montagne. He hadn't said anything about going into a café bar on the way.

'Tess?' Grant was waiting for me at the campsite.

'Hello,' I said.

'Where is everybody, Tess?' Grant asked. 'I tried phoning you, but your phone just rang and rang.'

I tried to sound brave, but it didn't really work. My voice came out all wrong. I sounded like a schoolgirl. 'I know. Maybe I ... left it somewhere. I'm not sure where.'

Grant didn't look surprised. 'Where's the group, Tess?' he asked again.

'They're having a cup of coffee,' I told him. 'And something to eat. At ... at the café bar in the village.'

'Having something to *eat*?' Grant repeated my words angrily. 'Having something to eat? What about their tents? You knew I wanted to show them how to put the tents up first.'

'But it's raining,' I said. 'They wanted to get dry.'

Grant was really angry. 'They'll want to be dry tonight too when they go to sleep!' he said. 'They won't be dry if they have to sleep out in the rain!'

'Well,' I said, '*we* can put their tents up.'

For once Grant agreed with me, but he didn't sound very happy about it. 'Yes,' he said, 'it looks as if we'll have to.' And he walked quickly away towards the Wild Country bus, which the driver had parked under some trees.

I followed more slowly, feeling a bit worried as I watched Grant get the tents out of the bus. I hadn't actually put a tent up before. But it couldn't be too difficult, could it?

It was. Within minutes of getting my first tent out of its bag, everything had gone wrong. The tent was very large, and I couldn't tell which way round it went. While I was trying to find out, the wind caught the tent, and soon it was over my head like a big, wet blanket.

'Oh!' I cried, fighting to get it off.

Grant came to help. 'Do you actually know what you're doing at all, Tess?' he asked. But he could see by the look on my face that I didn't.

'You've never led any camping tours before, have you, Tess?' Grant said.

'No,' I agreed, 'I haven't.'

'Have you even been camping before?' he asked.

'No,' I said.

'Well,' said Grant, 'you'd better watch and learn then.'

So I watched Grant put five tents up. Then he watched me while I tried to put the last one up. And all the time it was raining, raining, raining. I've never been so wet outside of a bath in my life.

'No, not like that; like this!' Grant told me impatiently when I did something wrong. 'Do it the way I showed you!'

'I'm trying my best!' I told him angrily.

'Are you really, Tess?' he said, taking the tent from me to show me again.

'Yes, I am!' I said.

'If you'd told the group they couldn't stay in the café bar, we wouldn't be doing this at all!' Grant said angrily, his hands busy with the tent.

I knew it had been weak of me to give in to the group, but I didn't want Grant to know that. 'They were wet, and they're on holiday,' I said. 'I wanted them to enjoy themselves.'

Grant turned to look at me. 'Well, I tell you,' he said, 'if I wasn't teaching you how to do your job better, then I'd tell you to do just that!'

I looked at him. 'What do you mean, just that?'

'I'd tell you to enjoy yourself,' he said. 'Forget about being a tour leader and just take a holiday.'

It sounded good, but as it was Grant's idea, I couldn't possibly agree. 'You don't think I could lead this tour on my own, do you?' I said.

'No,' Grant said. 'I don't. And neither does your father, or he wouldn't have sent you to learn from me.'

'My father's wrong,' I said. 'You're both wrong. I could easily lead this tour. Why don't *you* take a holiday, and *I'll* be tour leader!'

The sixth tent was finally up. Grant stood up and looked at me. 'OK,' he said.

I looked back at him, surprised. 'OK what?' I asked.

'OK,' he said again. '*You* be tour leader, and I'll take a holiday.' He threw me the keys to the bus and began to walk away. 'And I'm going to start my holiday with a good meal in the village. See you tomorrow at breakfast.'

'But …' I said, but he just gave me a wave without stopping.

'Bye, Tess,' he said over his shoulder.

I stood there, watching him go. *Now* what had I done?

* * *

When I got back to the café bar I found that most of the group had drunk wine with their meals. They were still sitting by the fire, and they were loud and happy.

'Tess!' Ellen said loudly when she saw me. 'Everything OK at Les Montagnes des Pins?'

'Les Pins de Montagne,' I told her unhappily, my stomach feeling very empty at the smell of the food in the café bar. 'Yes, your tents are all up. Maybe we'd better go now before it gets dark.'

But no-one was interested in leaving, so I stopped trying to be a good tour leader and ordered something to eat. And then everybody had some more wine. By the time we finally got back to Les Pins de Montagne, it was almost midnight. It took us quite a long time to find our tents in the dark.

As we walked around, Ellen, James and Sarah were laughing.

'Shh!' I said, trying to be a good tour leader again. 'People are trying to sleep!'

For some reason that only seemed to make them laugh even more. 'Shh!' they all said loudly. I thought I heard a loud cough come from Grant's tent.

But finally everybody was safely in their tents and I could take my wet clothes off. I was tired, cold and a bit worried about the next day. Would Grant really do what he'd said? Take a holiday while I acted as tour leader? I put on my nightclothes and got into my sleeping bag. Well, if Grant wanted to play games it was fine by me. I knew we needed to get packed up quite early the next day. But it must be easier to take a tent down than to put one up. Everything would be fine.

Chapter 7   *Asking for help*

But you can't take a tent down when somebody's still sleeping in it. And at nine o'clock the next morning nobody seemed to want to get up. Across the campsite, Grant was finishing his breakfast. He smiled and gave me a wave.

'Morning, Tess,' he said. 'Sleeping in, are they? Oh dear! Let me know when you're ready to leave, will you?' And then he lay down on the ground and put his hat over his face.

I wanted to run over and knock his hat off his face, but I didn't. I went into Ellen's tent and gave her a shake.

'Ellen!' I said. 'It's time to get up!'

'Mmm?' she said sleepily. 'What time is it?'

'Nine o'clock,' I told her, but Ellen had already gone back to sleep.

I left her to sleep a little longer and went to try David. I called his name, but he didn't hear me, even when I put my head inside his tent. There was a lot of soft laughing coming from Sarah and James's tent, so I didn't like to go in there. Only Astrid was awake, and she looked as if she hadn't slept all night.

'I will get up in a moment, Tess,' she said in her sad voice.

Astrid's tent was close to where Grant was. As I came out of her tent I heard him say something from under his hat.

'Pardon?' I said, going closer. 'What did you say?'

Just as Grant took his hat off his face, I fell over a stone on the ground. I ended up almost on top of him, and our faces were suddenly very close. Too close. 'I asked if you needed any help,' he said softly, and for some reason I couldn't stop looking at his mouth. It was a very nice mouth. I'd always thought so, right from the first time we'd met. And suddenly I was remembering how it had looked when he'd kissed the French woman beside the bus.

'Tess?' he said.

'Er … what?' I said dreamily, looking into his brown eyes.

He smiled, and I suddenly felt he knew what was in my mind. 'I asked if you needed any help to get everybody up,' he said, still in that soft voice. 'I was angry last night. We don't have to do this.'

'Do what?' I asked stupidly. It was difficult to think about what he was saying.

'This,' he said. 'This game. Let's forget about last night. I'll go back to being tour leader.'

I was mad, seriously mad. This was *Grant Cooper*. Grant Cooper, who enjoyed making my life as difficult as possible. Grant Cooper, who loved to make me look stupid. What was I doing looking at his mouth and thinking about kissing him?

'No!' I said, getting quickly to my feet. 'It's OK, thanks. I want to be tour leader.'

'OK,' Grant said. 'But if you change your mind, you only have to tell me.'

'No chance!' I thought to myself. As I walked quickly back over to Ellen's tent, I was sure I heard Grant laughing.

We finally left Les Pins de Montagne an hour and a half later than planned. It was dry, but the sky was full of dark clouds. It looked as if it would start to rain again soon. I don't think I was the only one who wished we were travelling in the bus with the luggage. We were a quiet group as we walked along; there was no laughing or telling jokes this morning. Most people were tired, and some had headaches from last night's wine. The only person who seemed to be happy was Grant. He was out in front, singing a little song to himself as he walked.

I certainly didn't feel like singing. We were going up another long hill, and my legs hurt. I was also remembering how I'd felt back at Les Pins de Montagne. How was it possible to want to kiss somebody and to want to push them off the hill all at the same time? Because I had wanted to kiss Grant. But I was *very* pleased I hadn't.

'Excuse me, Tess.' I realised David had come to speak to me.

I smiled at him. 'Yes, David?'

He looked uncomfortable. 'Well, it's just … Are you sure we're walking the right way? Only Grant told me we should go between those two mountains, and we seem to be going away from them.'

I stopped and looked across at the mountains he was talking about. Then I looked down at my map. Oh, no! David was right. We'd gone the wrong way several kilometres back. I'd been so busy thinking about Grant that I'd missed our turning.

'Problem, Tess?' Grant asked with a smile, coming back down the hill.

I tried to smile. 'No,' I said. 'At least, not really. We need to go back a little way. Sorry, everybody.'

Nobody said anything, but I knew they were a bit fed up. Especially David, who found going downhill difficult. Why hadn't Grant said something at the time? He'd obviously known we'd gone wrong. The man was acting like a child, and it wasn't fair to the group. We needed to talk.

I walked more quickly to catch up with Grant. 'This is stupid,' I told him when I got close enough to speak.

He turned to look at me. 'What's that, Tess?' he said with a smile. Oh, how I hated that smile!

'Why didn't you tell me we'd gone wrong?' I asked.

'You didn't ask me for help,' Grant said, walking on. 'You're the tour leader; I didn't like to tell you what to do. But as I said, if you do want help, you only have to ask.' And with that he walked on more quickly. There was no way I could keep up.

* * *

But if I thought things were bad, worse was to come. When we were high up on a mountain with no trees near, it began to rain again, very hard. We all had our raincoats with us that day, but the rain was falling so hard even they couldn't keep us dry. It was time for lunch, but there was nowhere to stop, and it was difficult to see where we were going. I wasn't even completely sure where we were. I had a picture in my mind of us still being up on the mountain in the rain by the time night came. I knew I needed help to get everybody safely down.

Feeling a little sick, I walked up to Grant. 'Can you help?'

'What's that?' he said.

I'd spoken quietly because I hadn't wanted anybody else to hear, but I knew Grant had heard me. He just wanted to enjoy hearing me say it again. But I had no choice. It didn't matter how *I* felt; what mattered was that everybody in the group was safe.

'I don't think I can do this,' I said. 'I think we're lost. I …
I need your help.'

Grant looked at me. 'Say please,' he said.

I wanted to hit him. 'Please,' I said. 'Please can you help?'

He smiled. 'Of course I can,' he said. 'I told you. You only
had to ask. It wasn't so difficult, was it?'

It *had* been difficult, one of the most difficult things I'd
ever had to do. But it was worth it. Within ten minutes we
were eating our lunch under some trees which Grant knew
about. For the rest of the afternoon we walked the right way
up and down the hills with him at the front.

I walked at the back, happy to leave him to it. I didn't
even try to talk to anybody. I was busy with my thoughts,
which were about my dreams of becoming a full-time artist.
I had to do it. I *had* to. I was a bad tour leader, and that was
never going to change. I'd always be a bad tour leader. My
father would just have to understand. I'd tell him as soon as
we got back to Nice.

Chapter 8   *Funny pictures*

The next few days were much the same. Grant walked at the front, and I walked at the back. Grant had us up by eight o'clock in the morning, and ready to leave by nine. Every day we went up mountains and back down them again. We ate our lunch at one o'clock, and we rested at eleven o'clock and three o'clock. By six o'clock in the evening our tents were up, and at seven-thirty we ate dinner. Oh, and there was something else that was the same. It rained. Every day.

One afternoon Ellen was walking next to me. 'This holiday is no fun,' she said. 'It's more like work than a holiday.' She looked at Grant, who was at the front as usual. 'He may look good enough to eat, but he's just "Mr Clock" – do this at this time, do that at that time. And tonight it's going to be even worse. No toilets, no restaurants. I don't know whose idea this camping *au sauvage* was, but it was a stupid idea. I'm fed up, Tess. Can't you tell us some bad jokes? *That* was fun.'

I looked at Ellen – who I now thought of as my friend – and smiled. Maybe I did have something to offer the group. Something Grant didn't seem to be able to give them. 'I'll think of something,' I told Ellen.

Ellen smiled at me. 'Good,' she said. 'And while you're doing that, I'm going to have another try at making "Mr Clock" up there take it easy.'

I watched as Ellen walked quickly to the front to join Grant. It wasn't long before I heard them laughing.

But nobody was laughing very much by the evening. The place where we were to spend the night would obviously be beautiful on a nice evening. But it wasn't a nice evening. It was wet, and the moon was behind a cloud. Everybody ate dinner together in the cooking tent, but there wasn't very much conversation.

After the plates were cleared away and washed, I shouted to everybody above the noise of the rain on the tent, 'If anybody wants a caricature of themselves, I'm happy to draw one,' I said.

'What's a caricature?' Astrid asked.

'It's a picture that makes you look stupid,' Grant told her helpfully.

I gave him a dirty look. 'It's a funny picture,' I explained to Astrid. 'It does look like you, but if you have a bit of a big nose, I make it *very* big. Or if you have small eyes, I make them very small.'

Astrid nodded. 'I know. I've seen those in newspapers sometimes. No, I don't think I want one, thank you.'

Ellen stood up. 'Well *I* do.' She sat down in front of me. 'Come on, Tess. Make me look as stupid as possible. Anything for a laugh.'

I moved some of the lamps so I had enough light to see. Then I held my pencil in my hand and sat looking at Ellen while I decided how to draw her. The best thing about Ellen's face was her eyes. They were beautiful – warm and friendly. She was so full of life too. That was what I liked about her. Things were never boring when Ellen was around. Her hair was very alive – she had a lot of it, and I thought it must be very difficult to brush in the mornings. Suddenly I smiled to myself.

'You've thought of something, haven't you?' said Ellen, watching my face.

I smiled at her. 'Yes,' I said, beginning to draw, 'but I'm not sure you'll like it.'

'I told you,' Ellen said with a laugh. 'I don't care. Do what you like.'

'OK,' I said, 'but remember you said that!'

As I drew, everybody except Astrid came near to watch. I soon forgot about them as I thought about what I was doing. I'd remembered a little cat I'd had when I was a child – Messy, I'd called her. She'd had a sweet face, just like Ellen, and she'd loved running about and getting into trouble.

The picture took about five minutes to finish. 'There,' I said, holding it out to Ellen.

She took it from me and began to laugh. I'd drawn her as half woman, half cat, with lots of wild hair all over the place and a food bowl with chocolates in it. Ellen was always eating chocolate.

'That's very good, Tess,' she said. 'Just like me on a bad day!' And she passed the picture round for everybody else to look at.

'Me next!' said Sarah.

Even Astrid asked me to draw her picture in the end. Astrid's neck is quite long, and her eyes are large and sad, so I made her neck very long, and her eyes very large. When I gave the picture to her, she looked at it for a long time. Her face was so sad I began to feel worried.

Then finally she spoke. 'Yes,' she said. 'It is very good.' Then I saw that she was crying. Oh no, what had I done now?

'Oh, Astrid,' I said, 'I'm sorry.'

She shook her head. 'No,' she said, 'it's OK. It's just that Christian always loved my long neck. He said … he said it was lovely. Like the neck of a water bird …'

'A swan?' asked David, and Astrid nodded.

'Yes, a swan,' she said, and then she took her picture and walked sadly away, still crying.

After that, everybody felt a bit flat, and most people decided to go to bed. Soon only Grant and I were left in the tent.

'Well,' I said, standing up, but Grant put out a hand to stop me.

'Wait a minute,' he said. 'You haven't done a caricature of me yet.'

Chapter 9 *The river mistake*

I looked at Grant as he sat down in the chair opposite me. I didn't want to draw him, and I knew why. It was because I didn't want to spend all that time looking at him.

'Oh,' I said. 'You don't want me to draw you, do you? I was only doing it to keep everybody happy this evening.'

'And what's wrong with keeping me happy?' he asked with a lazy smile. I knew I had no choice. I'd have to draw him.

'Oh, all right then,' I said.

With all the other pictures, I'd started by spending some time looking at the person. I didn't do that with Grant. I began drawing immediately, and I only looked up at him when I had to. And each time I *did* look at him, *he* was looking at *me*. It almost felt as if Grant was the one doing the drawing.

'You're a good artist,' Grant told me suddenly, and I nodded, continuing with my work.

'Yes, yes,' I said. 'And I'm a bad tour leader. I know. You don't have to say it.'

'I wasn't going to say that, actually,' Grant surprised me by saying. 'Those drawings you did of everyone were very good, that's all. You're a good artist. Or are you one of those people who don't like people saying nice things about them?'

I couldn't believe it was Grant saying nice things about me, that was the thing. I'd always believed him to be an uncaring sort of man. Or maybe not uncaring exactly, but the sort of man who didn't notice or think about how other people were feeling.

'Why don't you work as an artist?' he went on. 'Isn't there enough money in it?'

'I don't care about money,' I said.

'Then don't you believe in yourself?' Grant went on.

'Yes,' I said. 'No. Oh, I don't know. Not enough, perhaps. Look, do you mind staying quiet? I can't draw very well if I'm talking.'

Grant smiled. 'OK,' he said. 'But you should think about working as an artist.'

I said nothing, and just got on with my drawing. But after a few more minutes I looked at my picture and shook my head. It was all wrong. It wasn't a caricature of Grant at all. I needed to start again. So I put the first picture face down on the floor and took another piece of paper.

'What was wrong with that one?' Grant immediately wanted to know.

'It just wasn't right,' I told him.

But that wasn't good enough for Grant. 'Let me see it,' he said.

'No,' I said. 'I told you, it isn't right. Now please be quiet; I need to … '

'I know,' Grant said. 'You need to think.'

I smiled. 'That's right.'

This time I sat for a while before I began to draw, looking at Grant's face and thinking. Grant was a very strong person, and he had a strong face. He liked to be the boss. He had to be the best, and he always thought he was right. As I looked at him, I tried to think what animals were like that. And then I began to smile to myself again.

44

'I don't think I like that smile,' Grant said, but I just went on smiling and said nothing, my pencil moving quickly over the paper.

'Here,' I said when the picture was finished. 'I hope you like it.' But I didn't actually think Grant would like the picture. So I got up quickly and went to the tent entrance.

'Tess,' Grant said behind me, 'come back here!'

But I didn't stop. I just ran out into the rain, laughing. I'd drawn Grant as two animals – half big cat and half bull, complete with a ring through his nose! Well, that was just what he was like!

I thought Grant might come after me, but he didn't. So I threw my drawing things into my tent and walked towards the trees by the river to find somewhere to go to the toilet. On my way I went past Astrid's tent. It was open, and the rain was getting in.

I looked in to see if she was there. 'Astrid?' I called, but the tent was empty. I closed the front of the tent to keep the inside dry, and continued walking towards the trees. To tell the truth, I was very worried about Astrid. She'd been really sad when she'd seen my caricature of her. I was so stupid. I always seemed to make her feel even worse about things, poor woman. Where was she now? It was still raining very hard. She would be wet through.

As I went into the trees, I looked around for her. 'Astrid?' I called softly. 'Are you out here?'

There was no answer, but suddenly I heard a noise. Something large had jumped or fallen into the water a few metres away. Now I was *really* worried. 'Astrid!' I shouted. 'Astrid!' And I hurried over to the river to take a look. But I could see nothing. It was too dark.

'Astrid!' I called again. When there was still no answer, I began to run back towards the tents to find Grant.

The lamps were still on in the cooking tent. I hurried inside. Grant was sitting where I'd left him, looking at one of my drawings.

When he looked up at me he knew something was wrong. The drawing fell to the ground as he got up. 'What is it, Tess?' he asked.

'It's Astrid,' I said. 'I think she's jumped into the river!'

Grant got up immediately. 'Come on!' he said, moving quickly past me. We both hurried back towards the woods and the river.

'Where did you see her go in?' Grant asked, taking off his jacket.

'Just here, I think,' I said, as he began to take off his boots and trousers. 'Only I didn't really see her; I just heard something …' But my words came too late. Grant had already jumped into the river.

I watched from the trees as Grant swam through the cold water. Then suddenly he was *under* the water. I put my hands to my mouth, feeling very worried for both Astrid and for Grant. Time and time again Grant went under the cold water looking for Astrid.

After a while, Grant looked at me from the river. 'I can't see anything,' he said tiredly. 'Are you sure it was here you saw her go in?'

I was beginning to feel terrible. 'Well, actually, the thing is …' I started quietly.

'What?' asked Grant. 'Speak up, Tess; I can't hear you.'

I coughed. 'Well,' I said a bit more loudly, 'I didn't *actually* see her go in at all.'

Grant looked at me. '*What?*'

'Well,' I said, 'I did try to tell you, but you …'

At that moment there was the sound of something getting out of the water further up the river. Grant and I both looked towards the noise. So we both saw – at the same moment – a very large, very wet dog, which was running through the trees towards us.

After the dog had gone, I looked at Grant. 'Sorry,' I said. But he said nothing, and began to swim towards me through the dark water.

He was still quiet after he'd got out and was putting his clothes on again.

'I'm sorry, Grant,' I said again, but he just walked away through the trees.

I hurried after him. 'I'll make you a nice hot cup of coffee,' I told him.

Finally he spoke. 'No, thank you, Tess,' he said. 'You'd probably fall over and burn me with it.'

I stopped trying then, and followed him sadly through the trees until we got to the tents. Astrid's tent was still closed. I watched as Grant got down on the ground to open it. 'Astrid?' he called softly, and the next second the quiet of the night was broken by the sound of a woman screaming.

'What is it? What do you want? Go away!'

'It's all right, Astrid,' Grant said quickly. 'It's me, Grant. I just wanted to …'

'Go away!' Astrid screamed again.

People began looking out of their tents to see what was going on.

'Astrid, please,' Grant said. 'I just need to …'

'No! I'm not interested in you, do you understand? Get away from my tent!'

'All right, all right!' Grant said, quickly closing the tent and getting to his feet. Then he saw everyone was looking at him. 'It's all right,' he said. 'You can all go back to sleep.' Then he looked at me. 'Talk to her, will you? After all, you started this.' And he began to walk away.

'OK,' I said, feeling fed up. He was right; I had started all of this. Why hadn't I stopped to think? Or checked to see if Astrid was back in her tent before I ran to Grant like a wild woman?

'Astrid,' I said, speaking through her tent. 'It's OK. Don't worry. Grant was just checking to see if you were safe.'

'That's what *he* says,' Astrid replied through the tent. 'But I have seen the way he looks at women.'

'No, really, Astrid,' I said. 'He was just …'

'Even *you*, Tess,' Astrid said. 'He looks at you that way too. You should be careful. Now, good night. I want to sleep.'

I stood up slowly. 'Good night, Astrid.'

After all that, I found it difficult to get to sleep. I'd made yet another big mistake. Because of me, Grant had jumped into a river for no good reason. And now Astrid thought he was a dangerous man. I would have to try to explain it all to her again tomorrow. But I wasn't sure she would believe me. What was it she'd said? That Grant looked at women? That he looked at *me*? Was it true? I hadn't seen him look at me like that.

There was something else I hadn't seen before as well. It had hurt Grant that Astrid was afraid of him. When he'd walked away, he hadn't just been angry, he'd been hurt. It was a side of him I hadn't seen before. And it made me think about him differently.

I turned over, trying to get more comfortable in my sleeping bag, but I still couldn't get to sleep. I was thinking about drawing Grant now – the first drawing, when I hadn't seen him as a big cat or a bull. I'd drawn him just as he was. A strong man, yes. A man who always thought he was right, yes. But a handsome man too. That was why I'd stopped working on that picture. It was because I thought it showed the way I felt about him.

'You like him,' a voice said inside my head, and suddenly I knew it was true. Grant often made me so angry I wanted to throw something at him. But as I got to know him better, I saw that he could be quite nice when he wanted to be.

I closed my eyes. 'Oh, no,' I said to myself. 'You *can't* like him like that. You *can't*!'

But I knew that I did.

Chapter 10   *An unnecessary mountain*

We were a fairly quiet group the next morning when we set off for the day's walk. Astrid didn't seem to want to talk to anyone. I saw that she was making sure she stayed as far away from Grant as possible. I still wanted to explain to her what had really happened. But it seemed a good idea to leave it for a while.

'What was all that noise about last night?' Ellen spoke quietly so the others couldn't hear. But I didn't want to talk to her before I'd had the chance to speak to Astrid.

'Nothing,' I said. 'It was all a mistake.'

'What sort of mistake?' Ellen asked.

I smiled at her. 'I think we should forget about it,' I said. 'Tell me about your job.'

Ellen looked at me. 'No, thank you. I came on holiday to forget about my job. You're no fun any more, Tess. You're getting as bad as "Mr Clock" up there.' And she walked away.

Oh dear. Still, I'd been a tour leader for long enough to know it was impossible to please everybody all of the time. However, it would be good to please *some* people *some* of the time. And at that moment everybody seemed unhappy. But at least it wasn't raining.

But because we'd all expected rain, we were all wearing our raincoats and lots of clothes. There were no trees on this part of the day's walk, and soon we were very hot under the burning sun. The mountains were very beautiful, but we were all too hot to enjoy them.

I caught up with Sarah and James. 'This weather's a bit of a change, isn't it?' I said, and Sarah smiled at me weakly.

'I think I liked the rain better,' she said.

'Sarah's feeling a bit tired,' James told me. 'It's tiring, walking up a mountain every day. We're beginning to think this type of holiday was a mistake for our honeymoon.'

'We met on a Wild Country holiday,' Sarah explained. 'That's why we came; we thought it would be nice. But actually we just want to be alone.'

'And not to have to get up early,' James added.

'Everybody's very nice,' Sarah said quickly. 'It's not that. But nobody seems very happy.'

I knew just what she meant. I wasn't feeling very happy myself after last night.

'Well,' I said to James and Sarah. 'Couldn't you stay in a hotel somewhere for a few nights and meet up with us later?'

'We thought of that,' James told me, 'but we can't afford it. We're buying a house soon, and we need all our money for that. Although we'd still like you to paint us a picture, Tess.'

'Yes,' said Sarah. 'Of the mountains.'

I smiled at them. 'I'd love to,' I said. 'You'll have to give me your address. I'll send it to you when I've done it.'

'That would be great,' said James.

'But in the meantime,' I said, 'I'm sorry you're not enjoying your holiday.'

Sarah smiled. 'Oh, we'll be OK. Don't worry about us. We can always have a second honeymoon later on.'

'When we're old and grey!' James smiled, and Sarah laughed.

'Sitting in our armchairs and looking at the mountains out of the window!'

When James kissed her, I dropped back to leave them alone. They were a really nice couple. I liked them a lot. I wished I could do something for them.

Up ahead, I saw Ellen was talking to 'Mr Clock'. Grant hadn't said more than two words to me today. Was Ellen having more luck with him? Probably. But then she hadn't made him jump into a river, had she? I thought back to the evening in the cooking tent, before everything had gone so badly wrong. It had been fun, drawing Grant, with him saying nice things about my work. He'd meant it too, I knew. He really did think I was a good artist. And it meant a lot because he had said it.

This morning at breakfast, although I'd sat quite a long way away from Grant, I'd seen every little thing he'd done. The way he held his spoon, the way he put sugar in his coffee – everything. Things were different today. I didn't know what to say to Grant any more. I couldn't just be me any more. I felt like a schoolgirl who likes a boy in the same class as her. And the sad thing was, I knew Grant would just laugh if he knew how I felt.

Up ahead, I heard Ellen and Grant laughing. As I looked up at them, I saw Ellen touch Grant's arm. When Grant looked down at her with a smile, I knew Astrid was right. Grant liked looking at women. Just one girlfriend wasn't enough for him. I'd better forget all about Grant Cooper.

By the middle of the afternoon, I saw the village we were going to stay in that night down below us at the bottom of the mountain. But to my surprise Grant didn't begin to walk down towards it. He started to lead the way up another – very high – mountain.

'Stop, Grant!' the old Tess said in my head. But the new Tess said nothing. She felt almost afraid to speak to Grant. It was stupid, I knew, but I didn't seem to be able to do anything about it.

I was feeling quite fed up actually. I was very hot, my legs hurt again, and I was tired of watching Ellen and Grant together. She was still touching his arm when she spoke to him, and they were still laughing together all the time. I was so busy with my dark thoughts that I didn't see that the sky had grown dark too. Before we'd reached the top of the mountain it had started to rain heavily. Within moments we were wet through.

'Oh no!' said Sarah as we all hurried to put on our raincoats. 'This is a terrible holiday!'

Grant and Ellen had waited for us. 'It's not far to the top,' Grant said. 'Then we can go back down to the village and put the tents up.'

Everybody looked at him. David was the one who finally spoke. 'Are you saying we didn't have to climb this mountain?' he asked.

'No,' said Grant, 'we didn't really have to come up here. But we were early, and you can see a long way from the top.'

We all looked over the side of the mountain. All we could see was clouds and rain.

'On a good day, anyway,' Grant added. 'Come on,' he said, and continued walking up the mountain.

I wasn't sure everybody would follow him, but they did. Nobody looked very happy when we got to the top. And when we began the walk down, I saw that David's leg was hurting him.

After we'd put the tents up in the rain, everybody stayed in their own tent for a while to rest and change their clothes. I lay down and listened to the sound of the rain. I was very tired and I think I went to sleep for a while, because the next moment I heard somebody – a woman – shouting, and it woke me up.

I sat up to listen. It was Ellen. She was shouting at Grant. 'Oh, yes you did!' It had stopped raining now, and I could hear her very well. 'Don't try to get out of it. You've *showed* me that you like me as a woman. You were laughing in that special way and looking at me like that all day. What's the matter? Aren't I pretty enough for you? Do you only like women with long blonde hair or something?'

Grant said something, but his voice was quieter than Ellen's, and I couldn't hear him.

But I could certainly hear what Ellen said in reply. 'That is not true, Grant Cooper! Everybody knows you tried to get into Astrid's tent last night! Well, good luck to her, that's what I say! She's welcome to you!'

And with that, I heard Ellen leave Grant's tent and run to her own. Then everything was quiet. At least it was quiet for a few minutes, and then I heard someone else leave their tent. When he gave a small cough, I realised it was David.

'Excuse me, Grant,' he said. 'Can I have a quick word with you?'

This time I could hear what Grant said in reply, because he didn't try to speak quietly. 'Why not? Everybody else seems to want to. I'll come out.' I heard the sound of Grant's tent opening. 'What is it, David?' he asked.

'It's about this afternoon's walk. I didn't want to go up a mountain that we didn't need to go up. Why didn't you tell us? We want to choose. I don't think it's your job to choose for us. As leader you should …'

'I tell you what,' said Grant, sounding angry. 'I won't be the leader any more, OK? Tess can be the leader. I can see you all like her much more than you like me.'

I put my head out of my tent in time to see Grant walking away. He gave me a quick look. 'Did you hear that, Tess? Over to you.' And off he went.

Chapter 11 *An important phone call*

Nobody felt like cooking that evening and Grant hadn't come back. So we walked in a quiet, unhappy group to the village to find somewhere to eat. There was only one hotel, but it looked nice enough, so we went inside. There was a free table by the window, so we sat at it and looked at the menu. It was still quite early and there weren't many people in the restaurant. Perhaps that's why I noticed the woman behind the bar through the open restaurant door. *It was the woman from the flower market – the woman with the white shoes.* Difficult to believe, I know, but it was true. It *was* her, and she seemed to own the hotel. Well!

'Excuse me,' I said to everyone. 'I won't be a minute.' And I went over to speak to the woman with the white shoes. I'd thought of a plan to help Sarah and James.

Now that the woman wasn't angry about her shoes, she was actually quite nice. Her name was Marie. She was certainly surprised when I told her about my idea, but after a while she agreed to it. I was really pleased. At least one good thing might happen today.

I was just returning to the table to share the good news with Sarah and James when the door opened. Grant came in. When he saw us, he looked as if he might go out again. But there was nowhere else to eat in the village. 'It's all right,' he said, walking past us. 'I'll go over there out of your way.'

And we all watched as he crossed the room to sit on his own in a corner. As he picked up a menu and started to look at it, he looked really unhappy.

'The further away the better!' said Ellen.

'Yes!' agreed Astrid.

As for David, Sarah and James, they all just looked fed up. And suddenly I'd had enough. 'Now look, you lot,' I said, sitting down in front of them. 'This just isn't fair. You're being horrible to Grant.'

'He asked for it,' said Ellen, 'acting like that towards me and Astrid. And making David go up all those mountains when he didn't have to!'

I looked at her coldly. 'And is it Grant's fault it rained as well?' I asked. 'Or that this is the wrong holiday for some of you?'

'Well ...' Ellen began, but I didn't let her finish.

'No,' I said. 'Just listen to me for a minute, all of you.' They all looked at me. Nobody spoke.

'Astrid,' I said, looking at her, 'you were wrong. Grant came to your tent to check that you were OK, that's all. I was worried about you last night; you seemed so sad. I thought you had ... Well, it doesn't matter now what I thought. I was worried, that's all. I didn't know where you were. I told Grant about it and he tried to help. *Nothing else.*'

Next I looked at Ellen. 'Grant tries to be friendly to everyone; it's part of his job. From what I heard, you thought it meant more than that. You're a lovely woman; I'm sure lots of other men will be interested in you. If Grant isn't interested in you in that way, that's no reason to hate him.'

'But …' Ellen started to say, but once again I didn't give her the chance to finish.

'David,' I said, looking at him next, 'you're right. Grant *should* let you choose not to go up a mountain if you don't have to. But on a sunny day it would be beautiful up there.'

David nodded. 'That's true,' he said.

'Sarah and James,' I said, moving on.

They looked at me. 'What have we done wrong, Tess?' Sarah asked, sounding worried.

I smiled. 'Nothing,' I said, 'except choose the wrong holiday. But I've found a way to put that right. At least for a couple of nights.'

'How?' James asked.

'Yes, how, Tess?' Sarah added.

My smile grew even bigger. 'Marie,' I said, nodding towards the hotel owner, 'has agreed to let you stay here in the hotel for two nights. She has a nice double room you can have.'

Sarah and James looked worried. 'But we told you before, Tess,' James said. 'We can't afford to pay for a hotel.'

'You don't have to pay,' I told them. 'The room won't cost you anything.'

'But why?' Sarah asked.

'Marie and I have met before,' I said. 'I painted a picture of her. She hasn't seen it yet – it's back at the hotel in Nice – but she liked the drawing I showed her. She wants to put the picture up in the hotel. I said she could have it if she let you have a room here.'

Sarah smiled. 'Oh, Tess!' she said.

'We can't let you do that,' James said.

I smiled at them both. 'I want to do it,' I said, and then I stood up. 'Now, if you'll all excuse me, I'm going to sit with Grant.'

I walked away from them, feeling very good that I'd sorted everything out. On the other side of the restaurant Grant was still looking at the menu. Then suddenly I saw the hotel phone in the bar behind him and changed my mind. Grant could wait for a little while. I had to speak to my father. If I could talk to the group like that, then I was strong enough to speak to my father as well.

Dad answered almost straightaway. 'Tess? How lovely. How are you? And how are you getting on with Grant?'

It wasn't an easy question to answer at that moment, so I didn't try to.

'Everything's fine, Dad,' I said. 'Except …'

'Except?' he said.

'Be brave, Tess,' I told myself. 'Be brave!'

'Dad, I don't want to work for Wild Country any more. I'm really sorry, but I can't do it. I can't take over from you. I need to do work that's right for me, and working for the company just isn't right for me. I'm going to be a full-time artist.'

* * *

'Hi.' After my phone call I went to sit at Grant's table. He was still looking very fed up.

He looked at me for a moment, then went back to studying the menu. I thought he must know everything on it by now. 'Well done,' he said flatly.

For a moment I thought he was talking about the conversation I'd just had with my father. 'Well done for what?' I asked.

'For winning of course,' he said. 'People like you better than me, so you're clearly a better tour leader than I am.'

I sat and looked at him. I wanted to reach out to push the hair away from his eyes. He wasn't like a big cat or a bull at that moment. He was more like a little boy. 'It was never about winning,' I told him. 'Anyway, I get lost, remember?'

'You keep people happy,' he said.

'But I can't make them get up on time in the morning,' I replied.

'You help them to enjoy their holiday,' he said.

'You help them to climb mountains they didn't know they could climb,' I said.

'I *knew* you were the type of person who didn't like people saying nice things about them,' Grant said, finally looking at me.

I smiled at him. 'OK, thank you for those nice thoughts,' I said. 'And it's true, I am good with people in some ways. But I'm *not* good at organising them, and a good tour leader has to be able to do that. I'm not even good at organising myself. That's what I've just been telling my father.'

Grant sounded surprised. 'You've spoken to your father?'

I nodded. 'Yes, just now. I've just told him that I don't want to work for Wild Country any more.'

Grant's eyes opened wide. 'You're leaving?' he said. 'I can't believe it.'

'Why not?' I asked. 'You were the one who told me I should be an artist. That's what I'm going to do.'

'Are you sure, Tess?' Grant sounded worried now. 'I know I said that, but you shouldn't listen to what I say. I don't know anything.'

'Yes,' I said, 'I'm sure. It's what I've wanted to do for ages. I just needed to be brave and take that first step. You helped me to do that, that's all. I'm going to go to art school to study painting.'

Grant thought about it for a moment. 'Well,' he said, 'if you're really sure, then well done again! That's great. What did your father say when you told him?'

I made a face, remembering the conversation. It hadn't been easy for me to do it. I hated disappointing my father, but talking to him hadn't been quite as difficult as I'd expected it to be either. 'That's why it's taken me so long to say what I want,' I said to Grant. 'Because I didn't want to hurt Dad. But he was OK about me being an artist, really. He said he'd been waiting for me to say something for ages. He didn't want to talk about the future himself, because he wanted me to be sure I knew what I wanted. But that's why he put you and me together on this tour. Because he thought seeing someone who was good at the job would help me decide what I wanted to do. He knew that when I was really sure about being an artist, I would be brave enough to speak to him.'

'Good old Dad,' I thought now. 'How well he knows me.' And suddenly I felt like crying.

Grant saw that my eyes were wet. 'What's wrong?' he asked. 'I thought you'd be happy.'

I took a handkerchief from my bag and blew my nose. 'I am,' I said. 'Very happy. I've got what I wanted, haven't I?'

Grant suddenly looked very serious. He took my hand across the table. 'And is that all you want, Tess?' he asked. 'To be an artist?'

My face was suddenly red. I wanted to turn away from him, but I made myself look into his eyes. 'No,' I said. 'I want … I want us to be friends. That is … that is, if you want that too.'

Grant didn't speak for a while. He just sat there looking at me. 'No,' he said at last, 'that isn't what I want at all.'

I looked at him, feeling suddenly afraid. Had I really made him as angry as that? So angry he didn't even want us to be friends?

Grant still held my hand. Then he began to smile, and I allowed myself to begin to hope that maybe, just maybe, everything would be OK.

'Tess,' he said, 'you're a terrible tour leader and you often drive me mad. You make me jump into rivers and get us lost in the mountains in the rain!' Still smiling, he let go of my hand and reached out to touch my face.

'But the reason I don't want to be your friend,' he went on, 'is because … I like you. I really like you. And I want you to be my girlfriend.'

Chapter 12   *Mademoiselle Van Gogh*

It was so hot that the mountains were a smoky blue against the deep blue of the Provencal sky. Down below me, a field of flowers was dark purple against the orange buildings of a little village. I knew I'd have to go soon, so I worked quickly, trying to make the right colours with the paints I had with me.

Then suddenly I felt a strong hand on my shoulder, and somebody kissed my cheek. 'Come on, "Mademoiselle Van Gogh",' said my boyfriend. 'We've got to get moving.'

I put my paintbrush into the water and turned to kiss Grant on the mouth. 'OK, OK, "Mr Clock",' I said.

There were shouts behind us. 'Come on, you love birds! Lunch is over! We've got mountains to climb!'

It was the summer holidays and I'd returned to Provence to work as a tour leader for Wild Country again. Or at least *half* a tour leader, because Grant was the other half. He organised everybody, and I kept them happy.

We're a good team.

Cambridge English Readers

Look out for these other titles at Level 3:

Two Lives
by Helen Naylor

In the small Welsh village of Tredonald, Megan and Huw fall in love. But is their love strong enough to last? Death, their families and the passing years are all against them.

The House by the Sea
by Patricia Aspinall

A married couple, Carl and Linda Anderson, buy a house by the sea to spend their weekends. But one weekend Linda does not arrive at the house and Carl begins to worry. What has happened to her? Who is the taxi driver that follows Carl? And how much do the people in the village really know?

Just Good Friends
by Penny Hancock

It's Stephany and Max's first holiday away together and they want to get to know each other. They go to Italy and stay at Stephany's friend Carlo's flat in a Mediterranean village. But Carlo's wife is not very happy to see Stephany – and the two couples find out why, and a lot of other things about each other, in a hot Italian summer.

www.cambridge.org/elt/readers